W9-CXU-252

The Great Shape Caper

Written by Gary Miller

Illustrated by Catherine Deeter

It is a quiet morning at the Bones Detective
Agency. Sherlock Bones has curled up in his chair
for a nap. His helper, Dr. Dockson, is reading
a magazine.

Suddenly there is a knock at the door.

At the museum, the detectives search for clues.
Sherlock Bones finds claw marks on the wall.
Dr. Dockson discovers a cat whisker on the floor.

"This can only mean one thing, Bones," says
Dr. Dockson. "Miss Kitty, the yellow-striped
cat burglar, has struck again!"

5

Suddenly FiFi picks up a small, square card from the window ledge. "Could this be another clue?" she asks.

Dr. Dockson reads the card aloud: "Bowser's Junk Shop. Beagle Square."

Sherlock Bones and Dr. Dockson rush to Beagle Square. They have never seen such a place! Almost everything in Beagle Square is square. But outside the junk shop they find a metal triangle.

"This must be another clue!" Sherlock Bones exclaims.

7

At the Cat Box Café, Sherlock Bones and
Dr. Dockson meet a mysterious cat. She seems
to know what they want.

"Only Mr. Circle can help you," she says. She
hands them a circular piece of paper. It has
Mr. Circle's address written on it.

The detectives find Mr. Circle quickly.
Mr. Circle invites the detectives to sit down.
When they do, he shouts to his guards.
"Seize them. Lock them in the dungeon!"

Sherlock Bones and Dr. Dockson try to escape,
but they can't. Soon they are prisoners.

Dr. Dockson is worried, but Sherlock Bones just smiles.

"Those cats forgot what dogs do best. Dig, Dockson! Dig!" Bones cries.

In no time at all, they tunnel their way out of the dungeon!